The Lion Who Couldn't Roar

By
John Powers

Illustrated by
Alan Colavecchio

Ambassador Books, Inc.
Worcester • Massachusetts

Library of Congress Cataloging-in-Publication Data

Powers, John, 1949-
 The lion who couldn't roar / by John Powers.
    p. cm.
 Summary: Two unlikely friends, Theodore the lion cub and Hew the lamb, go on an adventure of friendship, faith, and understanding, as Theodore grows into his voice.
  ISBN 1-929039-10-7
  [1. Lions--Fiction. 2. Sheep--Fiction. 3. Animals--Infancy--Fiction. 4. Lost and Found possessions--Fiction. 5. Animal sounds--Fiction.] I. Title.
  PZ7.P883445 Li 2002
  [E]--dc21

                         2001006959

Published in 2002 in the United States by Ambassador Books, Inc.
71 Elm Street, Worcester, Massachusetts 01609
(800) 577-0909

Printed in Korea.

For current information about all titles from Ambassador Books, Inc. visit our website at: www.ambassadorbooks.com.

Dedicated to the children of Haiti, ministered to by Passionist, Priest and Physician, Fr. Richard Frechette, C.P.

Once upon a time, in a far away jungle, there lived a family of brave and beautiful lions.

Theodore was the youngest cub. He had learned how to walk and purr and growl just like all the other cubs. But there was one thing that Theodore could not do.

Theodore could not roar.

Day after day, Theodore tried to roar.
And day after day he failed.

Theodore's father showed him how
to take a deep breath and throw out his chest.
His mother taught him how to hold his mouth
just right.
But no matter how hard he tried, Theodore could not roar.

6

"I'll never be able to roar," Theodore said sadly.

"Of course you will," his father replied. "All lions can roar. When God created lions, he gave us all the gift of roaring."

"Maybe God didn't give me the gift," Theodore said.

"Yes, Theodore, God has given you the gift," his father answered. "You just have to learn how to use it."

7

All the other cubs laughed at Theodore and made fun of him.
"Theodore can't roar! Theodore can't roar!" they shouted.
It made Theodore feel different and dumb.
"I used to have so much fun running, playing, and purring," Theodore
said to himself, "but now everybody laughs and pokes paws at me.
"I've tried and tried and tried, but no one here can teach me how to
roar. Maybe if I go into the jungle, someone there will teach me."

Theodore said goodbye to his parents and friends and went off to the jungle.
The animals he met there did not care that Theodore could not roar.
They only wanted to play.

One day, as Theodore chased a beautiful butterfly around a big rock, he bumped into a little white ball of fluff.

Both the ball of fluff and Theodore landed with a thump.

Theodore jumped up angrily and demanded, "What are you?"

"I'm a lamb," the fluff answered. "My name is Hew. What are *you*?"

"I'm Theodore, King of the Jungle," Theodore growled, "and you knocked me over."

"I'm sorry, but I didn't see you," Hew said. "I've never met a lion, and I've been told to run as fast as I can whenever I hear one roar.

"But I have never heard a lion roar. Can you roar for me?"

Theodore's head sunk to the ground. His face turned red, and he pawed the dirt.

"I don't know how to roar," he said.

"Sure you can. You're a lion. All lions can roar," Hew said.

Theodore shook his head. He took a deep breath, thrust out his chest, opened his mouth wide, and pushed the air out as hard as he could.

But not a sound came out.

"See?" he said.

"Gee, Theodore, that's too bad," Hew said, "but I have my own problem. I'm lost and I can't find my way home."

Hew's face lit up. "I have a great idea! Let's be friends, and that way..."

Theodore interrupted him. "We're too different to be friends. I'm a mighty lion and you're just a fluffy little lamb."

"We aren't that different," Hew said. "We are both looking for something. I want to go home and you want to find out how to roar. If we become friends, then we can help each other."

And so, Theodore and Hew became friends.

They set out to find the sheepfold for Hew and a roar for Theodore.

Suddenly, a monkey screeched from atop a tree.

"Who are you and what do you want?" the monkey asked.

"I am Hew, Lamb of the Pasture, and this is Theodore, King of the Jungle. I am trying to find my way home and Theodore wants to learn how to roar," Hew said.

"Mr. Monkey, do you know how to roar like a lion?" he asked.

15

"Of course I do," the monkey squealed. "I hear lions roar all the time. And when I do, I quickly climb the nearest tree."

"Can you show my friend Theodore how to roar?" Hew asked.

"Certainly," said the monkey. "A lion sounds just like me, only louder."

The monkey threw his arms in the air, jumped up and down on the limb, and squealed and screeched as loudly as he could.

"WOO-WOO-WOO-HE-HE-HE. WOO-WOO-HE-HE-WOO."

"That's not a roar," Theodore growled. "I know what a real roar sounds like, and that is not it."

"Well, Mr. Monkey," Hew said, "even though you can't roar, perhaps you know the way to the sheepfold."

"I'm sorry," said the monkey, "but there aren't many trees to swing on in the sheepfold, so I have never bothered to go there."

"Thank you anyway," Theodore said, and the young lion and the little lamb continued on their journey.

Next, Theodore and Hew spied a snake sunning herself on a big rock.
"Excuse us, Ms. Snake," Hew said, "but could you help my friend and me?"
"Yes-s-s," said the snake. "S-s-since you didn't run away when you s-s-saw
me s-s-sunning mys-s-self, I'd be s-s-so very happy to help you."

18

"Do you know how to roar like a lion?" Hew asked.

"Of cours-s-se," said the snake. "I've heard many lions-s-s roar in my days-s-s of s-s-slithering through the gras-s-s. A roar s-s-sounds jus-s-st like this-s-s."

The snake lifted her head high and hissed, "S-s-s-s-s-s-s-s-s-s-s-s-s-s-s."

"That's not a roar," Theodore said. "Lions do not hiss! But maybe you can still help us. Do you know the way to the sheepfold?"

"S-s-sad to s-s-say," said the snake, "I don't know the way to the sheep-fold. I s-s-stay s-s-safely in the depths-s-s of the jungle."

So Theodore and Hew left the snake and continued along the path.

Soon they came to the edge of a river where a group of elephants splashed and sprayed and rolled in the mud.

A big gray elephant was swaying gently on the river's bank. Slowly, Hew approached him.

"Excuse me, Mr. Elephant. Can you help us?" Hew asked.

The elephant flapped his big ears at the tiny lamb. "What did you say?" the elephant asked. "Speak up! I can't hear you."

"Do you know how to roar?" Hew bleated as loudly as he could.

"Snore?" the elephant yelled. "You want to know how to snore? I know how to snore. Just ask the other elephants and they will tell you that I am the best snorer in the herd."

The elephant lifted his trunk, flapped his ears, snorted, and blew, making a sound like nothing Theodore or Hew had ever heard before.

"That's strange," Hew whispered to Theodore, "he has big ears, but they don't seem to help. Let's go."

21

As dusk settled in, the two friends were very tired and very sad.

They had tried all day, but Theodore still could not roar, and Hew had still not found the sheepfold.

When they felt they could go no farther, they came upon a cave. They lay down with heavy paws and were soon fast asleep.

But their troubles were not over.

A wolf crept into the cave. He looked at the sleeping friends, licked his lips, and growled.

Hew's eyes shot open and he sat up wide awake. He was face to face with the hungry green-eyed wolf. Hew was so scared that he bleated as loudly as he could.

Theodore awoke and stared at the wolf.

"What are you two doing in my den?" the wolf snarled.

"This is your den? We're sorry, we didn't know." Theodore explained. "We were tired and cold from our travels in the jungle. You see, I'm searching for an animal to teach me how to roar, and my friend needs to find the way to the sheepfold."

23

The wolf howled with laughter. "A lion who can't roar? Why, that's as funny as a bee that can't sting, or a fish that can't swim!" Theodore lowered his eyes and stared at the floor of the den.

"I can help you both," the wolf sneered. "I can teach a lion how to roar. And I certainly know the way to the sheepfold."

"You do?" Hew asked excitedly.

"Of course! It's just a little farther down the path. It's right next to the river," the wolf said.

The young lion winked at the little lamb.

"But not so fast," the wolf growled. "Suppose I do help you. What do I get in return?"

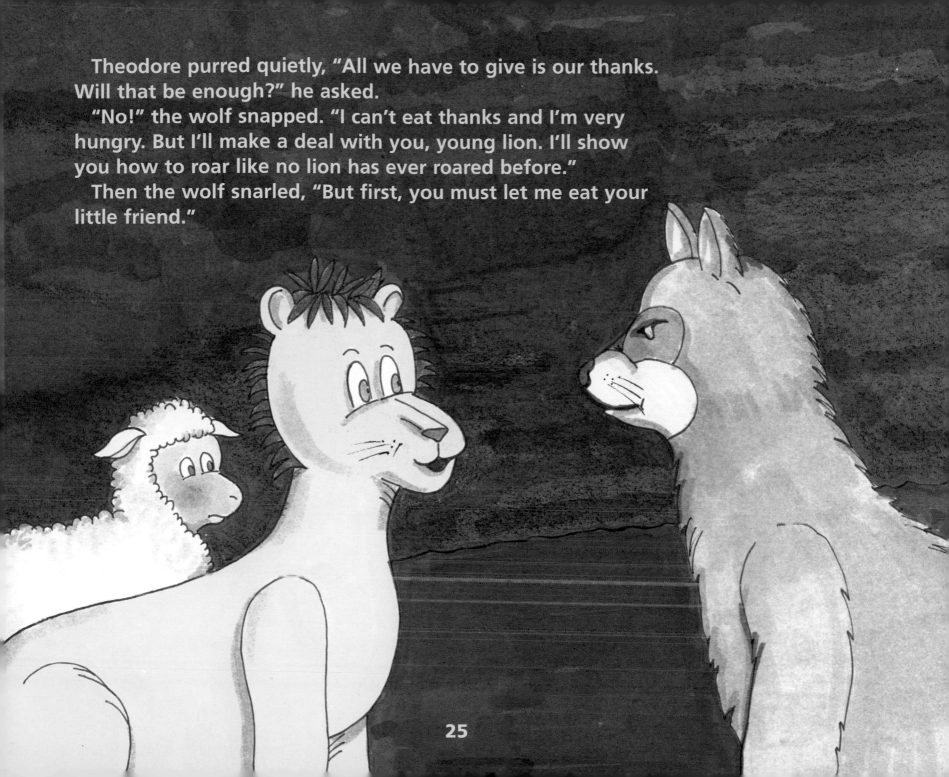

Theodore purred quietly, "All we have to give is our thanks. Will that be enough?" he asked.

"No!" the wolf snapped. "I can't eat thanks and I'm very hungry. But I'll make a deal with you, young lion. I'll show you how to roar like no lion has ever roared before."

Then the wolf snarled, "But first, you must let me eat your little friend."

25

Theodore trembled.

"No! No way! You cannot eat my friend for dinner!"

"Who's going to stop me?" the wolf howled. "You don't know how to roar like a real lion, and you're too afraid to bite my tail. I think I'll take my chances and eat your little friend."

The wolf showed his sharp fangs and glared his hungry eyes at Hew.

Hew froze with terror. "I'm going to be the wolf's supper," he thought.

The wolf snarled and inched closer to Hew.
Suddenly, Theodore stopped shaking, and something marvelous happened.
Theodore's fear turned into anger.
And his anger turned into a furious love.
He forgot that he could not roar.
He forgot that all the other lions had made fun of him.
He forgot about everything except his little friend.

27

Theodore felt a rumbling deep inside of him.
It grew bigger and stronger and stronger and bigger.
And as it grew, it rose to Theodore's throat.
It burst up into the young lion's mouth.
Then it bounced off his tongue, and rushed
past his teeth.
And as the wolf was about to pounce on
Hew, Theodore opened his mouth wide—

ROAR!

The wolf stopped dead in his tracks. It was the mightiest roar he had ever heard.

"If his bite is as big as his roar," the wolf thought, "I'd better leave Hew for another time."

The wolf bounded out of the cave and disappeared into the jungle.

29

Theodore was surprised by his own mighty roar. He was delighted, too.

At last he was a real lion! At last he could roar!

And so he roared again—

ROAR!!

"What a mighty roar! You saved my life," Hew exclaimed.

"My father was right," Theodore said. "God gave me this wonderful gift, but I had to learn how to use it."

"It's been a great adventure," Hew said. "It's a shame it has to end."

"Well, I guess it's time to say goodbye," Theodore said.

The young lion wiped his big paw across his eyes, so Hew could not see his tears.

"Wait a minute," Hew said, "before we say goodbye, why don't we travel around the jungle. Maybe there are some other animals who are lost…"

"Or who don't know how to roar," added Theodore.

"What do you say, Theodore?" Hew asked. "Shall we help others as we have been helped?"

Theodore raised his head, threw back his mane and roared with approval.

ROAR!